Dear Parents:

Children learn to read in stages, and all children develop reading skills at different ages. **Ready Readers**™ were created to promote children's interest in reading and to increase their reading skills. **Ready Readers**™ are written on two levels to accommodate children ranging in age from three through eight. These stages are meant to be used only as a guide.

Stage 1: Preschool-Grade 1
Stage 1 books are written in very short, simple sentences with large type. They are perfect for children who are getting ready to read or are just becoming familiar with reading on their own.

Stage 2: Grades 1-3
Stage 2 books have longer sentences and are a bit more complex. They are suitable for children who are able to read but still may need help.

All the **Ready Readers**™ tell varied, easy-to-follow stories and are colorfully illustrated. Reading will be fun, and soon your child will not only be ready, but eager to read.

Freckles Sneaks Out

Written by Eugene Bradley Coco
Illustrated by Susan Marino

Modern Publishing
A Division of Unisystems, Inc.
New York, New York 10022

Meet Freckles.

He is a brown cat with black spots.

He lives in a big house
with many rooms…

...and many people.

But today,

Freckles is all alone in the big house.

There is no one in the attic.

There is no one in the den.

What is Freckles to do?

"Maybe I'll go outside,"
thinks Freckles.
Outside there are
many things to do.

First, Freckles slides on the grass.

Then he rolls around in a big ball.

Next he runs to the lake.

Splish! Splash!
Freckles swims.
What fun!

Now Freckles is off to the park.

He slides down the slide.

He swings on the swings.

He monkeys around
on the monkey bars.

GRRRRR

Suddenly, Freckles is hungry.
"It must be lunchtime,"
he thinks.

Maybe someone is back
in the big house.
Freckles runs all the way home.

Lunch is waiting for him.

Everyone is waiting for him.

They are happy to see Freckles.

Freckles is happy to see them.

Everyone has lunch.

Freckles does, too.

Freckles is happy.

He had fun outside.

Now he's ready for inside fun!